ALL
The *Wrong*
THINGS
EXPLICIT TABOO EROTICA

JUST PLAIN BOB

WARNING

This book contains sexually explicit scenes and adult language. It may be considered offensive to some readers. This book is for sale to adults ONLY.

Please store your files wisely where they cannot be accessed by underage readers.

* * * * * * * * * * * * * * * * * * *

About the Publisher

4Fun Publishing, a member of **BLVNP Incorporated**, 340 S. Lemon #6200, Walnut CA 91789, info@blvnp.com / legal@blvnp.com
NOTE: Due to the highly emotional reaction of some people to works of erotic fiction, any email sent to the above address that contains foul language or religious references is automatically deleted by our anti-spam software and will not be seen. All other communications are welcome.

DISCLAIMER

Please don't be stupid and kill yourself. This book is a work of FICTION. Do not try any new sexual practice that you find in this book. It is fiction and not to be confused with reality. Neither the author nor the publisher or its associates assume any responsibility for any loss, injury, death or legal consequences resulting from acting on the contents in this book. Every character in this book is over 18 years of age. The author's opinions are not to be construed as the opinions of the publisher. The material in this book is for entertainment purposes ONLY. Enjoy.

All The Wrong Things
Explicit Taboo Erotica

By: Just Plain Bob

© **Just Plain Bob 2015**
ISBN: 978-1-68030-621-7

I sat there and stared at her incredulously. It took a few seconds for what she had said to register and in those few seconds my mind went back in time.

I'd met Tanya Louise Marshall on the first day of school when I started the eighth grade. She had just moved to town and didn't know anyone in the class. From the first time I'd laid eyes on her I was lost. I introduced myself and she gave me a big smile and said that she was glad to meet me.

My eyes followed her everywhere she went and when school let out for the day I asked her if I could walk her home and she said that it was sweet of me to ask, but she was going with some of the girls she'd met that day.

That was just the first of a thousand rejections that I received over the next ten years. They were always nice and gentle refusals, but refusals none the less. When we graduated from college she took a job somewhere on the west coast and I went to work in the family business and did my best to forget Tanya.

* * *

Even though my mind was always on Tanya I didn't let my feelings for her get in the way of my dating others. I did have an active social life even if I wasn't having it with the girl I wanted to have it with. Pauline French relieved me of my virginity and Harlina Collins, Beverly Abbeg and Nancy Wilde saw to the furtherance of my sexual education.

A year out of college I met and married Nancy Neubert. The marriage only lasted two years. It ended when I caught her in bed with her high school sweetheart. It was a cliché. I came home early one day and caught Nancy and her lover in bed.

I was very civil about it and simply told him to get dressed and get out of my house and he dressed and left without a word. I told Nancy to pack a bag and go stay with her parents while I talked to an attorney to see where things would go from there.

She begged me to let her stay and told me that it wasn't what I thought it was. I laughed at that and she said:

"Its true baby; it wasn't what you think. I love you and you know I do. All that happened here today was closure. Closure for both Alan and me" and then she told me the story.

She and Alan had been a couple from the seventh grade on. By the tenth they were already talking about marriage after high school graduation. Alan felt that since they were going to get married anyway it wouldn't matter if they started having sex. Nancy told him no. She told him that she intended to go to her marriage bed a virgin. He kept pushing and pushing and she finally broke down enough to start giving him hand jobs. By mid-eleventh grade she had progressed to giving Alan blow jobs.

Alan still kept pressing and she promised him that she would give him more sex than he could handle once they tied the knot, but not before. He told her he was going to hold her to that promise.

During the summer vacation between eleventh and twelfth grades Alan's father took a promotion that required that they move eleven hundred miles away. Alan promised that he would come back for her as soon as he had his high school diploma and then he reminded her of her promise.

Nancy and Alan had stayed in touch all through the next year and then suddenly she stopped hearing from him and all her letters to him went unanswered. After a while she figured that he had found someone new and she got on with her life.

We met and married and then one day Alan showed up where she worked and they had a tearful reunion. Over lunch Alan brought Nancy up to date on what had happened to him. He and his mom and dad had been involved in a five car pile-up on I-5 and his parents had been killed.

He had survived, but was in a coma for nine months. When he had come out of it he had no long term memory. After a year in rehab and therapy his memory had come back and as soon as he was able, he had come back for her. He was bitter at finding out she was married.

They had lunch together a couple of times a week and according to Nancy she only did it because she felt so bad over thinking that he had found someone else and that's why he stopped communicating with her. Over one of those lunches he reminded her of her promise to him. She told him she couldn't because she was now married to me. He told her that she owed him for all the times she sent him home with blue balls and she kept saying that she couldn't.

Alan kept working on her and she decided that she would do it one time with him more to settle what she thought of as a debt than because of love. It would give closure to their interrupted relationship.

"I felt I owed him baby. After all he had been through he came for me only to find that I hadn't waited for him. It was only going to be the one time and you were never supposed to know about it. Honest to God baby it was only going to be the one time. I love you Frank and you know I do. Please try to understand and please, for God's sake, forgive me."

I told her she still needed to pack a bag and leave because I had a lot of thinking to do and I didn't need her around distracting me.

* * *

She went to stay with her folks and I spent a week thinking about the situation and in the end I decided to take a chance on Nancy. She came back home and then proceeded to do her absolute best to spoil me rotten and fuck me to death.

After a couple of months it occurred to me that she was trying too hard and I started thinking that it was her way to keep me from thinking about what she might be doing so I decided to do some checking. I could account for all of her time in the evenings and on the weekends, but then I remembered that she said that she had met her old boyfriend for lunches.

I took a couple of days off work and was parked down the block from where Nancy worked about a half hour before her lunch hour. Nothing happened on Monday, but Tuesday she came out of the building at twelve noon and I followed her to the Starlight Motel. She pulled up and parked in front of room 103 and sat there. Two minutes later a car with California plates pulled up next to her. Alan got out of the car, walked over to Nancy's car, leaned in her window to kiss her and then went to the office. He came back with a key and the two of them went into room 103.

I sat and watched the door to 103 until Nancy came out and then I followed her back to work. Once she went inside I went back to the Starlight and a fifty dollar bill got me the information that Alan Pendergast had a standing reservation for room 103 on Tuesdays and Fridays. I'd never heard of a specific motel being reserved so I asked if there was anything special about the room that would make it desirable and I found out that it was the only room with a hot tub. All of the odd numbered rooms on the first floor were supposed to have had hot tubs, but the builder ran into financial problems before the other hot tubs could be installed.

As I drove home a plan took shape in my mind. Surprisingly enough I felt no animosity toward Pendergast. All he had done was come back for the woman he loved. True, she was with another when he got there, but he loved her, wanted her and so he didn't give a rat's ass about me. I didn't doubt for a minute that part of the time he spent with her was spent trying to get her to leave me for him. The only question in my mind was why she didn't do it? It was obvious to me that she wanted to be with him. Why else would she be meeting him?

That evening Nancy was her usual amorous self and I went along with the program as I did again Wednesday and Thursday. Friday when she pulled up and parked in front of room 103, I was in place and ready to put my plan into action. As soon as the two of them were in the room I backed the U-Haul truck I had rented up next to Nancy's car and started unloading boxes. I'd rented the truck Thursday and had purchased seventy-five moving boxes. I left for work at my normal time Friday, but had only driven around the block and then waited for Nancy to leave for work. I went home and packed everything of Nancy's into the boxes. I packed up everything that we had bought because she wanted it and then I drove over to the Starlight and waited.

I unloaded the boxes as quietly as I could and then I stacked the boxes in front of the door of the motel room. It built a wall three boxes deep and the only way to get out of the room would be to tear down the wall from inside the room and that wouldn't be an easy task since the wall went higher the door to the room. They would have to wrestle a box out of the first row only to find another row behind it. The last thing I did was lean the bed frame, box spring and mattress that Nancy had cheated on against the box wall.

The last part of the plan would take place when the two of them had finally worked their way out of the room. They would find a process server waiting to hand Nancy an envelope and to tell her that she had been served.

I drove home and prepared myself for the meeting that I knew was coming. Such preparation being three fingers of Jack over ice. I didn't bother changing the locks on the house. Nancy's name was on the title with mine and her paychecks helped pay the bills. I doubted that we could co-exist until the divorce was final so it was likely that one of us would have to move out, but it wouldn't necessarily be Nancy.

The phone rang at 3:10 and in answer to my "Hello" I got a "Can I come home?"

"It isn't a home anymore Nancy, but yes, you can come to the house."

She walked in at 3:25 and the first thing out of her mouth was a cliché. "It isn't what you think baby. I can explain if you'll let me."

"Go ahead. It has been a difficult day for me and I could use a laugh."

"I love you baby; honest to God I do, but I also have strong feelings for Alan. He was so much a part of my life that yadda, yadda, yadda…"

I listened and let her run down and then I said, "What you are telling me is that you want us both since you can't seem to choose between us."

I think I saw just a glimmer of hope on her face before I continued, "Since you can't seem to choose I guess it is up to me to make the choice and I choose not to be married to a cheating whore."

I looked at my watch and then said, "If you hurry you might be able to get to Alan's place in time to fix him dinner."

"But baby I …"

"Just go Nancy. You are damaged goods and I want no part of you."

It was a pretty messy divorce since it turned out that Nancy was pregnant and I wasn't going to accept paternity until I could be sure that the baby was mine. It wasn't and because of that and a prenuptial agreement she had signed Nancy didn't come out of it all that well. The only surprise was that she didn't move in with Alan. He left town two months after I had her served and he didn't take her with him.

* * *

Three months after the divorce became final I was sitting at the bar in the Landing Strip Lounge which was my watering hole of choice. It was open mike night and a parade of would be standup comics was entertaining the crowd.

A girl I recognized as a clerk at the gas station/convenience store I occasionally stopped at was doing her routine and since I knew her well enough to say hi to I listened to her routine.

"A man said to his wife one day "I don't know how you can be so beautiful and so stupid at the same time.""

"The wife said "Allow me to explain. God made me beautiful so you would be attracted to me. God made me stupid so I would be attracted to you.""

That got a loud laugh and some foot stomping applause from most of the women in the audience and she continued on. The next one must have been for Bobby Denton because everyone knew about his penchant for blond jokes.

"A mathematician, a philosopher and a blond go to Hell and receive a challenge from the Devil. If they can stump him they can go to Heaven instead of being roasted by the fires in Hell. The philosopher goes first and asks the Devil a very hard question. The Devil smiled and said, "That the best you got?" and then rattled off the answer. The mathematician went next and the Devil instantly gave the answer. When it was the blonds' turn she took a chair and bored three holes in the seat. She sat down on the chair and she farted. Then she looked at the Devil and said:

"Now tell me which hole the fart came out of."

"That's easy. It came out all three of them."

The blond laughed at him and said, "No stupid. It came out of my butthole."

That one got a decent laugh and then she said, "One more then I've got to get home and get the kids to bed.

"In a dark and hazy room, peering into the crystal ball, the Mystic delivered the grave news to Laura.

"There is no easy way to tell you this so I'll just have to be blunt. Prepare yourself to be a widow. Your husband will die a horrible and violent death this year."

Visibly shaken, Laura stared at the woman's lined face, then at the single flickering candle, then down at her hands. She took a few deep breaths to compose herself and to stop her mind racing. She simply had to know. She met the Mystic's gaze, steadied herself and then asked in a quivering voice, "Will I be acquitted?"

That one nearly brought the house down and she blew kisses to the audience as Bobby Denton walked out to take the mike from her hand.

I had only meant to stop for one beer before heading for home, but I was enjoying myself so I decided to have another beer. That decision was to lead to a startling consequence. Bobby asked if there was anyone in the audience who would like to come up and take a shot at making the crowd laugh and a hand went up from a woman at table with four other women. Her back was to me, but just as my second cold PBR was set down on the bar in front of me the woman turned and my heart damned near stopped.

The woman was Tanya.

Time had not lessened the effect that she'd had on me since the day I first met her. She took the mike from Bobby and thanked him for giving her the chance to embarrass herself in public and then said:

"A nice, calm and respectable lady went into the pharmacy, walked up to the pharmacist, looked him straight in the eye and said:

"I'd like to by some cyanide."

The pharmacist asked, "Why in the world do you need cyanide?"

The lady replied, "I want to poison my husband."

The pharmacist's eyes got big and he exclaimed. "Lord have mercy! I can't give you cyanide to kill your husband. That's against the law. I'll lose my license! They'll throw both of us in jail! All kinds of bad things will happen. Absolutely not!! You CAN NOT have any cyanide!"

The lady reached into her purse and pulled out a picture of her husband in bed with the pharmacist's wife. The pharmacist looked at the picture and said:

"You didn't tell me you had a prescription."

That got her a big laugh and she followed up with, "The teacher gave her fifth grade class an assignment. Get their parents to tell them a story with a moral at the end of it.

The next day the kids came back and one by one they began to tell their stories. They were all the regular types of stuff; spilled milk and pennies saved and things like that. She came to Janie who was the last one to tell her story.

"Do you have a story to share Janie?"

"Yes ma'am. My daddy told me a story about my mommy. She was a Marine pilot in Desert Storm and her plane got hit. She had to bail out over enemy territory and all she had was a flask of whiskey, a pistol and a knife. She drank the whiskey on the way down so the bottle wouldn't break when she landed and then her parachute landed her right in the middle of twenty Iraqi troops.

"She shot fifteen of them with the pistol until she ran out of bullets, killed four more with the knife before the blade broke and then she killed the last Iraqi with her bare hands."

"Good Heavens" said the horrified teacher. What did your daddy tell you was the moral of this horrible story?"

"Stay away from mommy when she's been drinking."

The house went crazy and Tanya left the stage to a standing ovation. As I watched her walk back to her table I wondered if I should attempt to say hello, but I couldn't figure out how to do it. I didn't want to suffer the embarrassment of being dismissed in front of four women I didn't know. I decided to take a chance.

I called the waitress over and ordered a round for the five women at the table. When she delivered the drinks she told the women who had sent them over all five women looked over at me and two of them waved thanks and then they went back to talking. I really didn't expect anything, but I had hoped that Tanya would have shown some sign of recognition. It didn't happen so I finished my beer and got up to leave.

I was almost at the door when I heard, "Frank? Wait up Frank." I turned to see Tanya coming toward me. I stopped and when she got to me she handed me a piece of paper and said:

"Call me."

She turned and went back to her group. I looked at what she handed me and saw that it was a piece of a bar napkin with a phone number on it. I looked back at the table and saw four women looking at me with what I could only believe was astonishment on their faces. Tanya sat back down with them and it looked like the other four were all trying to talk at once. I turned and went home.

* * *

When I woke up in the morning the first thing I saw when I got out of bed was that piece of bar napkin sitting on the dresser with all the rest of the stuff I'd taken out of my pockets before I'd gone to bed.

There wasn't any doubt but that I was going to call Tanya, but when should I do it? I doubted that the number was her work number; the question I had was what number was it? A home land line or a cell? Should I wait until the evening and possibly end up playing telephone tag if it was a home phone and she wasn't there? Or should I call right away and possibly catch her before she went to work? If it was her cell and she was up and already on her way to work would she answer it? Or was she one who wouldn't talk on her cell while driving and would let the call go to voice mail. What if she didn't drive to work and took the bus? Would she answer it or prefer not to because she didn't want to talk with a bunch of strangers around?

As I stood there looking at that piece of paper while busily over-thinking things something my dad used to say when facing difficult decisions came to me. "No guts, no glory." I walked over to the bedside phone and dialed the number.

* * *

She hadn't lost whatever it was that drew me to her. My heart beat faster as she walked toward me. I stood up and offered her my hand when she reached the booth.

"So good to see you Frank. I'm delighted that you asked me to lunch."

"The pleasure is all mine Tanya."

She gave me a big smile when I said that and then she slid into the booth across from me.

"So what have you been up to since I last saw you" she asked.

"Working and trying to live the good life. You?"

"Working and trying to climb the corporate ladder."

"I seem to remember that you moved to the west coast when you graduated."

"I did and after a couple of years and a promotion or two I took a promotion that brought me back here."

"Been back long?"

"About three weeks. You married Frank?"

"Was. Not anymore. You?"

"Never took the step. Too locked into my career to find time for it and to be honest most of the men I met and dated turned out not to be worth a second look. Certainly not worth giving up my career for."

We got into talking about careers for a bit over lunch and when the plates were cleared away she said:

"Since you invited me to lunch I'll invite you to dinner. You free tomorrow night?"

I did have plans, but they went instantly out the window and I said I had nothing going on. She gave me her address and I told her I would pick her up at six. She gave me a thousand watt smile and told me she would see me then and we both went back to work.

* * *

Friday I was at Tanya's at ten to six and I sat in my car until two minutes to six and then I went up and rang her doorbell. The vision that opened the door took my breath away.

Over all the years in school that I yearned for Tanya I'd never seen her look the way she looked when she opened her door. Four inch 'come fuck me' pumps, mini-skirt and a blouse that showed enough cleavage to get lost in and that thousand watt smile.

She was dressed to build hard-ons and I knew that it wasn't accidental. I wanted to drop to my knees and beg her to be mine and I could tell that she knew it. I had to ask myself, why?

Nine years of smiling sweetly at me as she turned me down time after time and now she was deliberately trying to entice me? Why? "Shut the fuck up!" a part of my brain was screaming at the part doing the wondering. "Take it and run. Thank whatever gods that be that you are even here."

I offered her my arm and said, "Your chariot awaits my queen" and she laughed, took my arm and I escorted her to the car. I asked where to and she gave me the name of a trendy restaurant and told me there was no rush as our reservation wasn't until seven.

We made small talk on the ride to the restaurant. The usual stuff like "Have you seen so and so since you've been back" and "Have you kept in touch with any of our classmates" and she asked if I'd gone to the five year reunion. I told her that I didn't go and she told me that she had wanted to go, but was in Italy at the time.

When we got to the restaurant I checked us in with the hostess and told the girl that we would be in the bar when they were ready for us. We found an empty table, sat and ordered drinks and when they came and after we had taken our first sip Tanya said:

"You are dying of curiosity aren't you?"

I looked into her smiling face and said, "I can barely contain myself from shouting out 'Why, why, why?' Nine years of being pretty much dismissed by you and now you are, for lack of a better way of putting it, coming on to me? Of course I'm curious."

"It is really very simple Frank; I want you to marry me."

"You have got to be kidding me."

"This isn't a joke Frank; I want you to marry me."

To say that I was stunned would be a massive understatement. The girl I had pined for since the day I'd met her in the eighth grade was asking me to marry her. I'd asked her for dates a thousand times between the day I'd met her until the day we graduated from college and she had never, not once, said yes. We had never even dated and here she was sitting across from me and asking me to marry her.

Un-fucking-real!!!

I sat there with my drink halfway to my lips and stared at her speechless! Absolutely fucking speechless. She was smiling at me and she said:

"Say something Frank. Don't just sit there; say something."

I finally managed to get myself together and said, "Simple? You call that simple?"

"I'll admit that there might be some details to work out, but it has been done many, many millions of times so the formula is pretty much down pat. License, blood tests and then the ceremony."

"But we don't even know each other. God knows that for over nine years I tried to get to know you, but the bottom line here is that we just flat don't know anything about each other."

"What's to know Frank? You're a boy and I'm a girl and we are of legal age. And don't even try to tell me that you aren't attracted to me. Don't forget I saw your face when I opened the door to you tonight."

"I'll admit to that, but looks alone aren't enough as I very well know from my marriage to Nancy."

Before I could go any further the hostess came up to us and told us that our table was ready. As I walked slightly behind Tanya and the hostess I was looking at Tanya's ass move and thinking that if looks alone were enough I'd get us on a plane to Vegas that very night and have the deed done in a matter of days, but as I'd told Tanya in the bar I already knew that looks alone would not make a marriage. If I'd learned nothing else from Nancy I'd learned that.

As soon as we were seated and had ordered I took the bull by the horns and asked:

"Okay Tanya, just what is the story here? What is going on?"

"I don't know what you mean."

"Of course you do. I chase after you for nine years with absolutely no luck and then go four years without seeing you and suddenly after a forty minute lunch as our only date, if it could even be called that, you ask me to marry you. I might have been born at night, but it wasn't last night so what gives?"

Her face lost its smile and she said, "I just found out I'm pregnant and for reasons I don't want to go into right now I need to get married as soon as possible. I need to have a husband before I show and ideally it should happen so the date of the marriage and the arrival of the baby seem normal to people."

"What's wrong with marrying the father of the child?"

"I have no idea who he is and even if I did I wouldn't marry the low life son of a bitch."

"That brings up more questions that it gives answers and the one at the top of the list is why me?"

"You bought me a drink that night at the Landing Strip."

"How does that enter into it?"

"I've only been back here a little over two weeks and I haven't met any guys I would consider. There were a couple who might have worked if I would have had the time to get into a relationship and get to know them well enough to ask them, but I don't have the time. I need it to happen now. The night you sent me the drink I recognized you when the waitress pointed you out. My immediate thought was that the guy who had spent so much time chasing after me might jump at the chance to be with me."

"I might have jumped at the chance no questions asked if I hadn't already been married to a cheating spouse."

"What does that have to do with this?"

"Why after being married to a cheater would I want to marry a promiscuous woman?"

"What?!! Where did that come from?"

"From you. You've already said you are pregnant and don't have any idea who the father of the child is. To me that indicates a level of promiscuity that would make me doubt the long term fidelity of a relationship."

"That's a pretty rotten thing to say about a girl you don't know a whole lot about."

"Which brings us right back to what I said just after you asked me to marry you. We don't know each other and don't know anything about each other. What I do know about me though is that I'm not about to jump into the fire you might be after jumping out of the frying pan that was Nancy. And then of course there are those reasons that you don't want to go into."

"Am I right in making the assumption that you are not against a marriage, but you won't go into it blind, deaf and dumb?"

"No you are not. I wouldn't even consider thinking about it until I knew everything about it that there was to know."

She gave me a long look and then she shrugged and said, "I had hoped that after dinner we could have gone for drinks and dancing, but I guess the mood for that is shut. I don't want to discuss my situation out in public so if you will take me home I'll put on a pot of coffee and tell you the whole sad story."

* * *

We made the trip to her place in silence and when we were inside her place she told me to have a seat on the couch and she went into the kitchen to make the coffee.

I looked around the room and wondered why I was even there. I should have walked her to her door, kissed her on the cheek and then gone on home. But curiosity and the fact that I had crushed on her for so long drew me. I was remembering all the times she had turned me down when I heard her say something.

"What?"

"I asked if you used cream and sugar."

"Just cream."

She went back into the kitchen and returned carrying a tray that had a carafe of coffee, two cups and a small pitcher of cream. She set the tray down on the coffee table in front of the couch and poured us both a cup.

"I'll let you do your own cream" she said as she sat down in the easy chair across from me. I fixed my cup, took a sip and then looked at her and waited.

"It isn't a pretty story" she said, "and I don't come off looking too bright, but the plain fact is I was gangbanged at a promotion party. I don't know if I was drugged or I was just too drunk to know what I was doing. I don't know if it was rape or not. I do know that when it was over I was between a rock and a hard place. Two of the men involved were related to my boss who was the owner of the company. One was his oldest son and the other was his nephew.

"If I have hollered rape and then gone to the hospital for a drug screen, my career would have been over. I had busted my ass to climb the ladder and I had earned my promotion to district manager twice over. I made the decision to put the night behind me and chalk it up as one of life's hard lessons.

"It wasn't easy because four of the seven worked with me and they figured that since I'd done it once they could get me to do it again and they kept after me. I kept shutting them down, but it didn't stop them from keeping after me. I couldn't complain to management and claim sexual harassment because the gangbang would end up being brought into it.

"Fortunately, for me anyway, the district manager in the office here had to leave the company for personal reasons and I was asked if I would be interested in relocating and taking the position. It was a no brainer for me. I made the move and a week after I got here I found out I was pregnant."

"I don't see the problem. Being an unmarried single mom is almost common in this day and age."

"That brings me to the other thing I didn't want to get into. My family is about as straight laced as you can get. Unmarried and pregnant would get me disowned in a heartbeat and I know this for a fact. It happened to my sister and outside of me no one in my family has spoken to her in over six years."

"From a purely personal standpoint they don't sound like people that I would want to have anything to do with anyway. I could maybe see a father being an asshole, but a mother who would turn her back on the child she carried for nine months? And then raised? She must be a real piece of work."

"I don't want to go there. Suffice to say I need to stay on the good side of my parents."

"Why? You are a grown up now. An adult who can make your own choices and live your life the way you want."

"This isn't going to put me in a good light, but I am a bit greedy. My parents are extremely wealthy and I stand to inherit quite a bit when they pass."

"So you are willing to marry someone you don't know all that well just to get a couple of hundred thousands?"

"No Frank; I'm willing to do it for six to ten million."

"You have to be shitting me!"

"Not at all Frank; not even a little bit."

"You do have other options. You don't have to have the kid. Have the procedure and your family will never know."

"I can't do that Frank. I may be a bit greedy and sometimes not to bright, but I can't get rid of something that is now a part of me."

She looked at me quietly for several seconds and then asked, "Could you do it Frank? Get rid of a life you helped create?"

"It would never get to be my choice Tanya. If it were mine I would argue against it, but the ultimate decision gets to be made by the woman. It is her body so it gets to be her choice."

"There you go. I choose to have the child."

"Even though you might not be able to get a husband and end up losing your inheritance?"

"I said I was a bit greedy Frank, but I'm not fanatical about it. Sometimes hard choices have to be made and you have to live with the consequences. So how about it Frank? Want to help a girl out?"

"What would be the mechanics of it?

"What do you mean?"

"A year? Two? How about the form of the divorce? What kind of prenuptial agreement to keep me from being raped in the divorce? Things like living arrangements? How to behave in social situations? What kind of front do we put up?"

"Why are you talking divorce when we aren't even married yet?"

"Don't pretend to be dense Tanya. It is a marriage of convenience. A marriage in name only. There is no love or affection involved here. It isn't even a business deal. There is nothing in it for me other than doing a favor for an acquaintance."

"Nothing in it for you?" she said as she stood up and stripped. She stood there naked in nothing but thigh high stockings and high heels. "You call this nothing? You chased after this for years Frank and I saw the look in your eyes when I opened the door to you when you got here. You're going to turn it down now that you have a chance? And what's this crap about living arrangements? If we get married it will be a real marriage.

"If it will ease your mind to have a pre-nup write one up and I will sign it, but I'll tell you right now I'm as much against divorce as I am against abortion. Any divorce that happens will be because you went for it not me. There will not be separate rooms or separate beds."

As she talked I stared at the near naked woman and the sight had the predictable results. She noticed and said:

"I see part of you doesn't find the idea all that repulsive."

She walked over to me, bent and rubbed the lump in my trousers and said: "Come on Frank; follow me into the bedroom and let me show you what's in it for you."

* * *

It was an exhausting night and we ended up falling asleep snuggled up to each other. I woke up in the morning to the sound of the shower. I debated joining her, but decided not to.

I dressed and went to her kitchen and found that she had the same make of coffee pot that I did. I rummaged around until I found the coffee and filters and then I got a pot started. I saw she had bacon and eggs in her refrigerator so I pulled them out, found the frying pans and started to build a breakfast. I fried the bacon and then as I scrambled the eggs I thought back on the night.

I know that earlier I'd told myself that if looks alone were enough I'd have us on the next flight to Vegas and a quick wedding with an Elvis impersonator presiding, but I had known that looks weren't enough. But looks and the sex we'd had last night could do it. Tanya had been damned near insatiable and she had done things with me that no other female had ever done.

She had let me cum in her mouth and no other girl had ever done that for me. Not even Nancy. Nancy gave a mean blow job, but she would never go all the way. Tanya did and she swallowed. Another thing I'd never done was anal. I'd always wanted to try it, but never had a girl who would allow it. Nancy had flat out told me that she would leave me if I even tried it (If I'd known how we were going to end up I would have just taken it and watched her go). I didn't even have to ask Tanya. She asked me!

We started out missionary, switched to doggy and then went sixty-nine to get me ready to go again. I was on the bottom so when Tanya got me hard she just scooted forward and took me in reverse cowgirl. After a bit she turned and settled into cowgirl and when I got to where I had to get off I rolled her onto her back and finished.

We rested a while and then she said, "I'll get you back to standing tall and then I want you to take me in my pooper. Will you do that for me?" I asked her if she was sure and she said, "I want you to know how far I'm willing to go to make things worthwhile for you." She was tight, but she had KY and she talked me through it. I have to admit that I liked it. I liked it a lot.

As I added a handful of cheese to the scrambled eggs I was giving some serious thought to what Tanya had asked me to do. She came into the room and I told her that the coffee was ready and breakfast was almost done.

"Nothing fancy; just bacon and scrambled eggs with some cheese."

"You're hired. When can you start?"

I knew she was kidding and meant that I was hired as breakfast chef, but I decided to take it a step farther.

"Depends on how fast we can get the legal stuff out of the way."

"Legal stuff?"

"Yeah. Stuff like the prenuptial agreement, the license and blood tests and lining up someone to perform the ceremony."

"You'll do it? You aren't joking are you? You will really do it?"

"If you are willing to meet certain conditions."

"Conditions? What are they?"

"First and foremost is a pre-nup that will protect me when the marriage ends. Next is a written agreement that will penalize you monetarily if you cheat on me while we are married."

"I don't understand. Isn't that what the pre-nup is for?"

"No. All the pre-nup is going to say is that if the marriage ends, no matter what the reason, both parties walk away with what they brought into the marriage and that what they acquired jointly will be split evenly. The penalty agreement will see to it that I get a bonus for putting my life on hold for you only to have you go out and cheat on me."

"I still don't understand. Why are you already thinking of me cheating on you and we haven't even gotten married yet."

"Why would I expect you to stay faithful? We wouldn't be getting married for love. It is only a marriage of convenience. A way for you to stay tight with your family. You know nothing about me and after living with me for eight or nine months you may decide that you don't even like me. After the baby is born you might start looking for a replacement; someone more to your liking.

"I'll say right now and up front that I can see it happening and I'll also say up front that I have no problem with it as long as you are honest with me about it. What I will have a problem with is you doing your looking behind my back. If you do that you are bound to be found out. Even if it isn't by me it will likely be someone who knows me or who knows of me. The word will get out and I will have people looking at me and thinking all kinds of things about me from I beat you or cheat on you and you are getting even with me to I'm no good in bed and you are getting your satisfaction elsewhere.

"When I found out these things, and eventually I would, I would have to suffer the embarrassment and humiliation of dealing with the people who knew. The penalty agreement wouldn't make it go away, but it would definitely help assuage the bad feelings."

"So how much would this penalty be?"

"See my worry here? We aren't even together yet and you want to know what it is going to cost you to get rid of me."

"Don't be stupid Frank. I need to know so I can tell the attorney what to put in the agreement."

"I'll leave the amount up to you. You put in what you feel it should cost you if you cheat on me."

"So, pre-nup and penalty agreement. Any other conditions?"

"Two more. In public you will treat me as any loving wife would treat her husband."

"No problem there since I would do that anyway. What's the last one?"

"That I get at least two nights a week like the one I had last night."

"Only two? Was I that bad?"

"You were astounding."

"Then why only two?"

"Back to the beginning. We both know that this is a marriage of convenience. I'm giving up my freedom and to play it right I won't be able to go out and date and see to my sexual needs so I need to make sure that I lock them in ahead of time. Once again I need to point out that you might not even end up liking me enough to want to have sex with me. This last condition is to insure that whether you want to or not you will. The 'at least two' is a minimum. It should go without saying that I will take as much as I can get."

"There isn't any way I could give you a legal document that will cover that. Besides, an agreement like that couldn't be enforced."

"Doesn't need to be in writing and enforcement is simple. You agree to the condition and I hold you to it. You don't honor the agreement and I simply go public about the marriage and the reasons for it and the people that you wanted to hide things from would know what you didn't want them to know."

When I finished I could tell from the look on her face that things weren't going as she had expected (or hoped) so I asked:

"Do we have a deal?"

"She looked at me for a bit without saying anything and then she said:

"I don't have much choice. I need to get things done and done quickly. I don't have the time to date and find someone suitable that I could then ask."

She gave me another few seconds of silence and then asked, "Why? Why are you even willing to do it?"

"The simple truth is that I don't have anything better to do. That and the benefit of a sex life that will be regular and that won't cost me an arm and a leg."

"You don't have anything better to do?"

"After Nancy burned me I haven't had any interest in entering into another long term relationship. Mostly I just go to work and then go home. Friday and Saturday I go out to see what I can pick up to relieve my sexual tensions. I score some, but not enough. I can go through a couple of hundred a weekend on shows, dinner, drinks and dancing and still go home with a case of blue balls. This arrangement will save me money and give me the sex life I need."

The look on her face made me curious so I asked, "You having second thoughts now?"

She shrugged and said, "No; no second thoughts. It just isn't going the way I thought it would."

"Just how did you think it would go?"

"To be honest, given the way you chased after me during our school years I thought that you would happily jump at the chance and that would be it. I didn't expect the somewhat cold business-like way you have taken. It hasn't put me off; I just didn't expect it."

She paused and then said, "There isn't much we can do until Monday. We can apply for the license and do the blood tests Monday and I can see an attorney and get him going on the legal stuff. I think there is a three day waiting period so figure on next Thursday or Friday to tie the knot. That okay with you?"

"That will give us time to work out some of the other things that need to be looked at."

"Like what?"

"Like where we are going to live. Do you own this place?"

"No. It is a sublet. I've got it for two months while the owner is in England on assignment. It is only supposed to be temporary while I look for a place of my own."

"I kept the house in my divorce so unless you have an objection that is where we will live."

"I've no problem with that."

"Next we need to see my parents. I need to introduce you to them and they are going to want to know why we are rushing into things so I'm going to tell them that I got you pregnant and we need to do it in a hurry."

"What will they think of me? A woman having sex while not married?"

"They won't think anything of it. Mom will be overjoyed that she is finally going to be a grandmother. I'll leave it to you as to how and when we break it to your family."

"That is going to be the toughie. I can' use the "I'm pregnant and we have to get married" story. I think I'll tell them that we met at a party, fell head over heels in love and eloped to Vegas and got married. They won't be happy, but it will be a done deal. My mom will be pissed because she has been planning my wedding for years. I expect that she will get over it when she finds out I'm pregnant. She has been after me for years to get married and give her grandchildren."

"I thought she already had one. Didn't you say that your sister got pregnant?"

"She miscarried."

"That's a shame. Does she live close?"

"No. She moved to Georgia when my parents disowned her."

"We will have to go visit when we get a chance. Do you have any plans for the weekend?"

"I was going to go grocery shopping either today or tomorrow, but nothing other than that."

"That can wait. We can use the weekend to move you into my place and then you can check out what I have in the pantry and fridge before you grocery shop."

* * *

And that is just what we did. By Sunday afternoon Tanya was moved in and was making out her grocery list. We hit Safeway and got what she wanted and then stopped at Outback for dinner.

When we got home I called my mom and told her I was getting married again and asked when would be a good time to bring my bride to be over to introduce her to them. She told me to come to dinner on Monday.

Monday we applied for the license and got the blood tests. Tanya saw an attorney and he told her he would have the paperwork ready for signatures on Wednesday.

That evening we went to my parents for dinner. Dinner went well and mom and Tanya seemed to get along great. I could tell from the way that dad looked at Tanya that he approved of my choice, but he did pull me aside and asked me if I knew what I was doing.

"It hasn't been all that long since you divorced Nancy. Are you sure that this isn't an 'on the rebound' thing?"

I think I surprised the hell out of him when I said, "I'm marrying Tanya for the same reason you married mom. She is pregnant and I'm stepping up to the plate."

"How long have you known?"

"Years and years. I saw your marriage license when I was digging through your desk trying to find something. Paper clips I think it was. Given the date on it and my birth date it wasn't hard for me to put two and two together."

"Well then all I can say is that I hope you will be as happy as your mother and I have been."

Mom got me alone and said, "She seems like a lovely girl. I hope it all works out for you. I'd hate to see you go through another divorce."

"What will be, will be mom. But you have to remember that it wasn't love that got us here – it was lust."

"If you work at it love can come along and you can trust me on that."

On the way home Tanya said, "I like your parents. They seem real nice."

"They liked you too. My dad even told me to make sure I did everything in my power to hang onto you."

"Are you going to?"

"It is a two way street babe. It will take both of us."

We had made love every night since our Friday date and if sex alone could make it happen we would end up celebrating our fiftieth anniversary.

* * *

The paperwork was ready Wednesday afternoon and we signed and had the signatures notarized. Friday at eleven we were married in a civil ceremony with my parents as witnesses and embarked on our new lives as a married couple.

Surprisingly things went well. We learned all the things about each other that you usually learn during a courtship. We found that we liked the same foods, mostly the same music and the same authors. There were some areas where we didn't quite match. She was into chic flicks and I was more of an action thriller fan. She was an avid bridge player and I couldn't stand the game, but we both played pinochle, euchre and cribbage. We were both runners and fitness freaks and she joined the same gym where I worked out.

We had been married two days when she took me home to meet her parents. The looks they gave me when Tanya told them that we had run off to Vegas and had been married by an Elvis lookalike pretty much told me that I was never going to be in the top ten on their favorite people list. It was a stilted evening as you might guess and I was happy to get the hell out of there when Tanya said that we needed to be going.

"They will come around when their grandbaby arrives" Tanya said.

The next two months saw us having dinner or attending barbecues with relatives from both families so they could meet the bride and groom. At the affairs Tanya told everyone that she had gotten pregnant on our honeymoon. With the exception of her parents most of her relatives seemed to like and accept me and my side of the family took to Tanya and told me that I had struck gold. Strangely enough my parents and Tanya's parents got along great. Tanya was proven right and her parents did come around when they found out they were going to become grandparents. I still wasn't in their top ten, but maybe I'd moved up to eleventh place.

* * *

There were a few hiccups along the way. Tanya's job was taking up a lot of her time and there were a lot of late evenings and some weekend work. I got on her about it and she told me that she had worked her ass off to get where she was and she was going to keep working her ass off to make it to the next level.

"I'm going to be their first female vice president."

"How in the hell are you going to do that? You are going to have a kid to take care of."

"Day care. I'll work until the baby is born, take a short maternity leave and then go back to work."

I thought she was whistling Dixie, but she was going to do what she was going to do and I had no say in it.

Regardless of the hours she worked and how tired she was when she got home Tanya never slacked off when it came to our love life. I was getting way more than the twice a week I had insisted on. We were getting it on four, five and sometimes six times a week and two-thirds of the time Tanya was the aggressor and nothing was off the table. Tanya especially liked anal and her oral was state of the art right down to and including swallowing.

Our sex life did slow down some the closer Tanya got to her due date, but we were still averaging three times a week right up to the middle of her eighth month. At that point Tanya said no more until after the baby arrived and she was cleared by the doctor to have sex again. Well that wasn't exactly true. She did give me blow jobs and I got her off with my fingers right up till when her water broke.

She was at work when it happened and she took a cab to the hospital. She called me on her cell as the taxi hurried her to Saint Joseph's and let me know what was going on. My office was only three blocks from the hospital and I was already waiting at the entrance to the emergency room when her cab arrived. While I was waiting for her to arrive I called both sets of parents and brought them up to date.

When she got there she was rushed into delivery and after a four hour wait the doctor came out and told us mother and child were doing fine. We already knew from the ultra-sound that the baby was a boy and we had already picked out the name. My father in law was pretty much speechless when he and my mother in law went to the nursery to view their grandchild and found out that he had been named after my father in law. It was what Tanya wanted and I could not have cared less. I got a handshake and a thank you from daddy in law and a big hug from my mother in law which came as a huge surprise since it was pretty much the first time she had more than look down her nose at me whenever Tanya and I were around her. I think maybe I'm in seventh or eighth place now.

My folks showed up about a half hour later and they oohed and aahed over the baby and I almost felt guilty that the child was not really mine, but I had signed up to play the role so play it I did.

They had moved Tanya to a recovery room and as soon as the nurse told us we could visit, we all tromped in to visit her. She was lying there with little Jason Alexander in her arms and I swear that I had never seen a more beautiful sight in my life. Tanya smiled at me and held the baby out to me as she said:

"Meet your son Frankie."

I took little Alex from her and something happened. My figuring to be a pretend daddy went out the window as the baby's hand closed around my finger and gripped it. As he looked up into my face and gurgled I made a silent promise that I would be the best daddy he could hope for.

* * *

I picked Tanya and little Alex up at ten the next morning and took them home and once there I got them settled in. I'd taken the week off from work so I could take care of Tanya until she was able to get back on her feet, but that plan went quickly into the toilet. It seems that both grandmothers had gotten together and decided that it was up to them to take care of Tanya and the baby. I was pretty much chased out of the house by the two of them and I had no place else to go so I went back to work.

One thing was certain. If the grandparents had their way Jason Alexander Dalton was going to be one spoiled rotten kid.

The day after I brought Tanya home from the hospital Tanya woke me up with a blow job and when it was over I asked her why.

"It will be at least six weeks before we can make love again."

"Before I can make love again" she said, "But I have to get you off at least twice a week. That was the deal right?"

"Given the circumstances I'm not holding you to that."

"I'm holding me to it. Besides, I like giving you pleasure."

I decided not to argue with her.

* * *

The next two years slipped by. Tanya took four weeks of maternity leave and then the grandmothers went nuts when they heard Tanya was going to put Alex in day care and go back to work. No day care for 'their Alex,' at least not if they had anything to do with it. They worked out a schedule where they would alternate keeping Alex while Tanya was at work.

Professionally Tanya was doing well where she worked and had made the jump from district manager to regional manager and was now only one step removed from the vice presidency she was after. I was doing fine although I didn't have to fight my way up the ladder like Tanya had to. It helps when it is a family owned business.

On a personal note I found out that my mother was right. Love did come along if you worked at it and I did. Things were going along great and then one evening Tanya came home from work and told me that she had a problem. A very major problem.

One of the men who had taken part in her gangbang had transferred into her region and during their first meeting in her office he told Tanya that he wanted her to meet him at his motel to have a 'long lunch' with him as he put it. She told him to fuck off and die and he laughed at her and opened his briefcase, took out a folder and handed it to her. She opened it and found a dozen or so 8X10 photos of her being gangbanged. He then told her that she WOULD meet him at his motel or copies of the photos WOULD find their way to me and copies WOULD appear in every office in her region.

"He gave me until tomorrow to decide."

"I don't see a problem with it. Meet with him."

"Are you out of your fucking mind?!!!"

"Of course not" and then I went on to explain what we were going to do. She smiled at me and told me it made her hot just thinking about it and then she suggested that we spend some time in the bedroom before going over to her mom's and picking up Alex. I thought that was a pretty good idea and so we did just that.

* * *

His name was William Bagley and William was having trouble looking me in the eye. Maybe it had something to do with his condition. He was naked and sitting on one of our kitchen chairs. He was securely bound and only his right arm was free and he had a rag stuffed in his mouth. The chair was pushed up to the kitchen table and there was a pad of paper and a ballpoint pen in front of him. Also on the table in front of him were a soldering iron and a small butane torch.

How did Willie come to find himself in that situation? Tanya had called him into her office and told him that there was no way she could take off for a long lunch as there was too much going on in the office at the time and she needed to be there to handle it. She also told him that there was no way that she was going to meet him at his motel. She would not risk being seen by someone who knew her.

Then she told him that I was going out of town on business Tuesday and would be gone for three days and she would send Alex to her mother's for the night and that he could come over to the house. She set it up for Wednesday. That way she could be sure that I'd made my flight and wouldn't walk in on them.

When Willie arrived Tanya was naked except for a pair of 'come fuck me' heels when she opened the door and Willie had laughed and said:

"You slut! You want this as bad as I do."

Tanya smiled at him and told him to come in. He walked in and then fell to his knees when I came out from behind the door and nailed him in the kidneys with a baseball bat. I dropped the bat and put him in a choke hold until he passed out and then I stripped him and dragged him over to a kitchen chair. I manhandled him to the chair, secured him and then Tanya and I went into the bedroom and knocked off a piece.

When we came back into the kitchen we found Willie struggling to get loose from his bonds. Tanya and I sat down at the table across from him and I said:

"I'm afraid you have upset my wife Willie, and I'm the kind of husband that hates to see his wife upset and does whatever is necessary to rectify the situation. What we are going to attempt to do here tonight is remove the reason for her being upset."

I reached over and pulled the rag out of his mouth and he immediately started hollering for me to untie him.

"Not going to happen Willie. Not until you have done what we require of you."

"I'll have your ass in jail for this asshole."

I stood, backhanded him and then stuffed the rag back in his mouth.

"Here is the way it is going to go Willie. You are going to pick up that pen and write down where every picture you have of Tanya can be found and then you will write down the names of anyone else who has pictures of that night. You will do it or I will use the soldering iron to burn "Blackmailing Asshole" into your chest and then I will use the butane torch to roast certain parts of your body. Your choice Willie; the easy way or the hard way."

He sat there and gave me a hard look and made no move to reach for the pen. I shrugged, picked up the butane torch and lit it. When I started to move toward Willie with the flame hissing he suddenly grabbed the pen and started writing. When he was done Tanya read what he had written.

"According to this the only place he has pictures is on his laptop and he says that he is the only one who took cell phone pictures that night."

"Do you believe him?"

She shrugged. I took the rag out of Willie's mouth and said, "My bride isn't sure that you have been totally forthcoming Willie so I guess I'm going to have to apply some incentive."

I fired up the butane torch again and started to move it toward Willie's foot.

"I'm telling the truth damn it; honest to God it is all there."

I looked at Tanya and she shrugged and said, "We know where to find him if he lied."

I shut off the torch and said, "If you go to the police over this all it will get you is the jail cell next to mine. In case it slipped your mind blackmail is a crime."

Tanya placed a digital recorder on the table, hit the play button and Willie's meeting with Tanya when they set up the evening played.

"You do know that I don't want to do this right? The only reason it happened the first time is because the seven of you drugged me and then raped me."

"So what if we did? You have no way of proving it."

"Please don't make me do this. I really don't want to chance messing up my marriage."

"I don't care if you want to do it or not. You WILL do it or I will ruin your reputation and make you the company laughing stock."

I stopped the recording and said, "We don't need to waste time listening to the rest of the recording. There is enough on it to charge you so if I do go to jail so will you. Where is your laptop?"

"In my motel room."

While I entertained Willie Tanya took his keys, went to his motel room, got the laptop and brought it home. There were a total of twenty-one pictures on Willie's hard drive and I copied them onto a thumb drive and then deleted them off of his computer. It embarrassed Tanya that I saw them, but I needed to know a few things. I had her tell me who the men in the pictures were. She did and then I cut Willie loose and told him to get dressed and when he was done I handed him his laptop and said:

"If you lied and any of those photos show up three things will happen. One, the gangbang will be out in the open and I will see to it that the pictures I now have will get to your boss thereby exposing what you, his son and his nephew did to Tanya. He may not be too pleased to have his son and nephew called rapists. He might even fire you and see to it that you get a reference that will ensure you never get a good job again.

"That ties in with the second thing. There is no statute of limitations on rape and Tanya will press the matter. True, it will be her word against yours, but her word will be backed up by the recording we have and you will be dragged out into the public's eye. And don't think for one minute that she won't do it. Once you have put her photos out there for all to see she has nothing to lose in coming after you.

"It is the third thing that you need to seriously consider. I will hunt you down and when I'm done with you, you will wish that I had gone all the way and killed you. Do you understand me?"

He looked away from me and said, "Yes. Yes I do."

He left and as we watched him walk to his car Tanya said, "Do you think that we really got all of the photos?"

"No way of knowing, but I saw the look in his eye when I told him what would happen if any turned up. He believed me and I'm betting that if there are any he will destroy them"

"And if he doesn't?"

"You of all people should know that I am a man of my word."

"I'm not usually into porn, but looking at those pictures has given me some ideas. Care to follow me into the bedroom?"

She headed for the bedroom and I smiled and followed along behind her.

~~The End~~

WANT FREE COPIES OF MY BOOKS?
Just visit my blog and download free copies of my books:

My other BEST SELLING books available on Amazon!!

She Let Them: A Cuckold Husband Story

"Who does you best, you sleazy tramp?"

What do you do when you find out your wife is cheating on you?

Screw her over of course, with a vengeance.

But things don't always go so smooth for Henry and his plans. Is there something more to it? Why his wife was really cheating on him and what happened that led to it? Things are not always how they seem.

And now here comes another player to the game and everything just becomes a hot mess.

What this new player has for Henry will leave him in a pile of ashes when he finds out what she's keeping secret.

EROTICA: Fifteen Minutes of Ass, Legs and other Kinks

Rob catches his girlfriend Misty in bed with another guy...in his bed, in his apartment. Furious, Rob throws Misty out of the house.

But just before Rob gets over the incident, he receives an e-mail from Little Miss Sweet Cheeks. It's a picture of a bum in a pearl thong. Rob is aroused, but he can't help but think that perhaps his male officemates are just pulling his leg.

Rob tries to play it cool until Little Miss Sweet Cheeks says she's ready to come out in the open. But just as she does, Misty runs after Rob asking for 15 minutes to explain why she cheated.

Women! Can't live with them, can't live without them. What's Rob going to do about Misty and Little Miss Sweet Cheeks?

Read on as this book will make you boil with pleasure...

Those First Times: A Collection of six First Time stories

By: Dick Parker

It's different for everyone but every guy will always remember his first time…

It's sweet, it's rough, and it ends all too soon – but it's definitely a moment that will change you forever.

Here are six "first time" stories that will bring you back to those moments of innocent youth and uncontrollable desire and lust just before you give in to the pleasures of the flesh.

Everyone has a different story to tell and here you will read about 6 different young guys as they fumble and navigate through the mess that is – virginity.

There doesn't have to be love, there doesn't have to be attachment – just losing it.

This collection will get you reminiscing the feelings of Those First Times.

Brooke Likes it Soft: Taboo Lesbian and Bisexual First Times

By: Amy Redck

Brooke's journey to self-discovery begins when she finds out the pleasure of masturbation. With her momma giving her the talk and her pop giving her "toys," Brooke is ready to find out more about her body.

Her escapades include the husband of her momma's friend, Stevie, who slowly introduces her to oral pleasure and penetration. And then there's Carli, her best friend, who gets to share with her Peter, Brooke's "toy."

And there's Mischelle, Stevie's wife who is supposed to look after her while Brooke's parents are away. It is Mischelle who informs Brooke that she and her momma are lovers and her pop knows about it. Part of the challenges of growing up is self-discovery. Brooke is learning more about women and is soon realizing that women satisfy her intimate needs. Does this mean that she's a lesbian?

Read on and follow Brooke's journey to self-discovery.

Storm Warning: Taboo, MMF, Younger Woman

By: Jack Ryder

Jake has a new sexy neighbor, Zoe, whose hot body churns a storm inside him. They play a cat and mouse game from the time she moves in next door.

Zoe is a young and very gorgeous woman, and Jake feels he's too old for the likes of her. To top it off, Zoe buys lingerie for a man who has snagged her attention, and this only dismays Jake furthermore.

In his depression, he decides to contact Mona for a book signing tour. For 6 months, Mona serves as his companion, and more. And when he returns home and sees Zoe, the feelings are still the same.

That afternoon Zoe announces that there is a storm warning and decides to spend the night at his place to ride out the storm, and him. While the storm rages outside, a different kind of storm is raging inside his bedroom.

The next day is Jake's birthday, and without his knowledge, Zoe is cooking a surprise that's going to change his life.

The Next Customer

By: Dingus Guy

There are more perks to being a security guard at a spa than Don realizes.

He likes his job, and there are only a few instances when he has to throw people out of the Eden Spa and Resort. Like one time when he has to save Autumn, one of the clientele, from a drunkard's advances. He does not think much of her after that.

But fate is not done with them yet. The following morning, Don and Autumn meet again at the Jacuzzi while everyone is away. The talks turn to flirting, and Autumn effortlessly challenges him to attend a class of her choosing and in turn, she would attend a class he likes.

The class she chooses? No-touch tantra class. And both Don and Autumn find it hard to simulate making love without touching, with their naked bodies only inches away from each other.

Check out the list of all my books!

The Prodigal Family: The Abbotts

Watching My Shared Wife

The Waitress and the Runaway Husband

Baiting Mr. Little

Too Hot for Henry

Chuck's Fantasy

The Redhead's Desires

Rescued at Riley's

His Every Fantasy

Open Mike Night

Pursuit for Revenge

Why Does He Do That?

Halloween & Drugs

Tracey

When Rob Met Kari

Becoming a Shared Wife, Vol. 1 –
(Wife Sharing and Other Adventures)

Becoming a Shared Wife, Vol. 2 –
(Hazardous Wives)

Becoming a Shared Wife, Vol. 3 –
(Wives Who Stray)

Her Illicit Adventures

What I Want To Do To Her

Too Fun To Give Up

Creamed

Stepping Out

Hottest Wife

Naughty Wives

Deepest and Darkest

More Than She Can Take

Jennifer's Toes

The More The Sexier

Spice Up

Cyndi

Naughty And Nice

House Of Lovers

Hungry For More

Sweet Revenge

Turning Mommies Wild: The Carriage Tales

Bought And Used

Get Me Off

The Gambler

Gail's Price